THE MAN WHO DIED EN ROUTE

THE MAN WHO DIED EN ROUTE

Nell Altizer

The University of Massachusetts Press

Amherst, 1989

Copyright © 1989 by
Nell Altizer
Printed in the United States of America
LC 88-7581
ISBN 0-87023-645-8 (cloth); 646-6 (paper)
Designed by Edith Kearney
Typeset in Linotron Plantin at Keystone Typesetting, Inc.
Printed by Thomson-Shore, Inc.
and bound by John H. Dekker & Sons, Inc.

Library of Congress Cataloging-in-Publication Data
Altizer, Nell.
    The man who died en route / Nell Altizer.
        p. cm.
    ISBN 0-87023-645-8 (alk. paper). ISBN 0-87023-646-6 (pbk. : alk.
paper)
    I. Title.
PS3551.L7935M3 1989
811'.54—dc19   88-7581
                                                      CIP

British Library Cataloguing in Publication data are available.

FOR MAUDE AND SARA JANE

Lift me out of this mire; let me not sink
In pudled poole, from such whose thoughts can think
   But hatred to my soul
And from this bottomless, and banckless deep
   O save, and set me free.
Keep, that these streams orewhelms me not O keep
This gulf engulf me not, this gaping hole
   Shut not her mouth on me.

     Psalm 69, translated by Mary Sidney,
     Countess of Pembroke

Acknowledgments

The following poems (sometimes in slightly different form) appeared in these magazines:

Hanai: "Hunger"

Hapa: "Heather"

Hawaii Review: "St. Christina the Astonishing"; "The Man Who Died En Route"; "Haleiwa Churchyard"; "Demeter's Lament" Sonnets 4, 5, 6, and 8

The Little Magazine 11, no. 3 (Fall 1977): sonnets 1, 2, and 3 from "Fool, Said My Muse" (originally entitled "'The Solemn Songs' Five"). Reprinted by permission of *The Little Magazine*.

The Massachusetts Review: "Letter"; "Letter to Karma"

Prairie Schooner: "Haworth Parsonage, 31 March 1855"; "First Blood." Reprinted from *Prairie Schooner* by permission of University of Nebraska Press. Copyright © 1979 University of Nebraska Press.

13th Moon: "The Widow Suite"

Contents

THE MAN WHO DIED EN ROUTE

St. Christina the Astonishing

Afflicted with sainthood
and able to smell out grief
in the dying animal, spending
the rest of her little life in flight
from the rank evidence of God—
she who climbed out of the ripe
thirteenth-century air of green wounds and graves
far too frequent and shallow for fragrance
(pigs in the kitchen along with the sprouts
and the tripe)
into the haven of an oven
for the fresh breath of prayer—

took God's gift of dying young
with good grace. But what He kept back
in His teasing wisdom—
the odor of sanctity—pitched her,
rapt and offended, out of her coffin.
The celebrant, turning away from the *Dies Irae*
to see her wailing like a common
wench against the ceiling—
"I cannot *stand* (she cried) the rancor of my stench!"—
commanded her back to her box for the end of the requiem.

No saints visited with blistering hands
or burned sheer through the heart
with the coals of His terrible love
match the ardor of that
fair and fastidious soul descending
out of the air again
and down to its stinking dust.

Oh astonishing Christina, pray for us!

The Watch

Old people don't need much sleep
my mother said as I watched
from the upstairs window first light
chisel my grandfather's rockhard kneeling
out of the bloom of his champion roses.
And I would fall back down
into the flat sleep of tidepools
that at five I was recovering from.

Old people don't need I would dream
when fast asleep I heard the scratching
of his rake against the walk,
some great beast climbing patiently backward,
for day and night he was planting.

A sailor, his eyes were the color of fins,
blue to their very bones, and a scar
from the quick lash of an anchor chain
braided itself forever to the shin
he used for a cushion on the grass
as if in some vast church and he
the only worshipper there,
stooping when the small wounds
of Peace and Snowfire and Crimson Glory
broke through their dawn-white gauze
and when the middle of the night
rose and fell like breathing
out of the earth he has prepared.

Haleiwa Churchyard

The common hands of a girl
and woman I love as well as
grass on this good field

          lay their inquisitions
          like flowers over the years
          of the narrow dead.

Under us are oceans
of birds and spring roots
and the long sound of rain.

          One after one tonight
          while we lie miles
          from these travelers

the stars will wash the stone
calendars with silver water.

          So that our sleep is no
          more difficult than this

the old earth sails again

          toward its appearances.

The Widow Suite

1   The Widow's Luncheon

We open the gate for her at noon
when the sun like a parasol
is overhead and stunning. "Come in," we say,
our mouths drawn up with words as if with pins.
She is our sister, the car keys
ringing the last, left fingers,
the bottle of wine like a club in her hand.

Yellow tomatoes bulge out of the vines
glistening and waxy as babies.
Down from the roof of the toolshed the passion flowers
turn their spiked lavender timepieces backward.

We sit in the garden and speak of planting.
We say *seed* and *rainwater*
and *flower* and *leaf* and
cuttings and *pollen* and *sunlight*.
Our sounds pull the sallow fist from a cucumber's sleeve.

Later, we will compare our voices to
the wind in the foothills,
hazy and falling.
We do not say *dirt*, what its violence weighs.

Now she stands, her new shoes on her shadow,
leaning on nothing
not even our hunger.

Slowly she comes to the table we set
as if there were something to eat.

2   Widow Song

Little sister, should you marry
will you lose?

Little sister, would you
marry out of luck?

In the silence, in the hollow,
will you lie down in the pool

that the threads between
our fingers cannot cross?

For the straw, for the locks,
for the window, for the box,

little sister, for the night
pluck will you follow

in my shoes? Could you marry,
little sister? Marry loss.

3   *The Widow Teaches Writing*

Over and over again she orders her students
out to the graveyards to find their poems.

Any old line, she says, the slug, the kicked-down
pot, spurge, condom, wreath, the brace of geckos

in the weeds, the gravekeeper's cracked-toothed rake,
even (if you must) the long limousines of silence.

And you over there, yes, *you.* Tell me the
story of your Chinese grandmother's duties:

how after seven years she must dig
the bones of her husband's father out of the dirt

and wash them one by one in the clear rain
water and lay them to dry in the sun,

while her son's wife kneels down beside her
in the patient air to see how it's done.

The boys and girls come back sweating the words
that say, *shit.* You hard bitch.

Their poems reek fear and earthworms, faces
smeared with hate for her,   Dis,

who has brought them young and early, young
and twitching to this place.

4   The Mourners

"You never miss the tree until the shade is gone,"
Mother, her voice trailing
the same old willows, says to the wife
when they put him down.

Dad gnarls his mouth to a knot,
stands, blasted and stuck to his seersucker suit,
under the June sun.

What hangs over the box is green,
a limp wave toward the natural,
hard to imagine in such light—
this furnace-blue Missouri sky against
the grain of Carrara marble—
and in such a construction site.

But it is good dirt you rub
between your fingers, sizing it up:
clay, loam, leaf mold, some lime, some traces
still of silt from the river
and, baffling and warm as sex,
the old delta smell.

The sisters put their cotton gloves back on,
but the stain grows like a fortune
in their palms.

The walking back is always hard.
Nobody wants to step on a sleeping place
and women will
wear those shoes. So an arm
goes out and a hand.
"Here now," and "let me help you."

Like the beginning
of music when the cello strikes the tone.
Two or three halt,
and one turns back to look.
More gather, form a base
chord from the resin in our voices,

draw the dissonance in,
and with faces as determined as the stones around,
proceed, proceed,

whether there is shade or not
or trees.

For Lou (1927–1961)

Passio et Mors

Crepe myrtle and mourning doves
and the bees and constant purple
constantly light
on the plumeria trees.

Here little room for absence
or death or anything why
mountains bunch in cracks
their green and sleeping
bags of lizards why the ocean
low as it is
is the highway. Still

promptly at seven at this meridian
night so abruptly drops
its shroud there is no time
to think of Lazarus
or walking on water even
the small human
horror of miracles, of constant light.

Each night I raise my drink
in darkness to paradise
hung on the southern cross
and hear rolling away like a vast stone
always the sea.

Coda

Your body slept in time so long the last afternoon
I scale its glyphs under the spiral water
with a sponge to make it wash.

The house is empty: yellow in ladders
over the banister eddies,
andante, sky,
a blue shallow, and windows.
The bird's-nest fern unfolds another foetus beat of green.

Silence. The great falls of remembered
Mozart in my hands and shasta daisy lemon
pollen on the glass.
Water and skin and water and rind and light!

In the chamber you have entered and entered,
entered and left
like music
a cello spreads an unreflecting pool beside
the white on white on white on white on white.

The Man Who Died En Route

I

The man who died en route. Trying that imposture
gingerly, he huddles under the blue
blankets of United. And in lieu
of chicken soup, the chipped-nose flight attendant's demure
palm on his forehead, me feeding (as I've nurtured
kids with spoons) him smokes. Out of what friendly skies do
you guys come from with your briefcases and needs askew
on planes? Why, like our gear, do I still tilt and slur

the safe landing? Twice his eyes scale the fence
of his glasses to glimpse my biography
of L. M. Alcott. Twice again. Like an old friend
who has read for years in bed with me.
The glance strikes. Tires (not he) expire and clench
that first collision where the heart, stopping, bends.

"Perhaps you'll write a sonnet about the man
who dies en route," he says, pouring alka-
seltzer into his coffee not to cool but blah
it down. Perhaps I'll write a hundred goddamned
sonnets about the men who die, I *can*
say (don't). Two fortifying vodka bottles castle
my tray. Check and mate. He, later, to the stew, "Uh,
we're not together, but give my 'Princess Chicken'

to her little girl: they're on economy."
The man who might—when he's discovered
by his ticket to be flying economically—
have died of shame (and doesn't) hands Sara the cheese
sandwich that's our class. Saving and just as these brief
words, the man en route sighs deeply like the dead.

My mind, a sign painter, lines up the door:
Altizer, Blaustein, and Butterick: a firm
of dactyls. Or, as the man who still might die en
route, says when we skid: "three epitaphs." More
bolt upright in our seats than tombstones for
the surprised-to-be-judged dead, we confirm
the halter of prayer, of wording. When the burn
of rubber ("Don't worry," he says, "*I'm* here.") lowers

the white flag of my face to half mast: ("Dear,
I surrender"), who am I talking to?
We are all here, hearing. It's the night watch
man I'm after: the squint eye cast on glass and notch-
ing the names. That God, paint splattered, slow to
dissolve the partnership and make the door clear.

Suppose the man died en route to Maui,
his last breath curled like a heartworm in the orchid
of his mai tai? Suppose, without hibiscus red
blankets or body bags woven from ti
leaves or a burial cave for the debris,
Aloha Airlines had to dispose of a dead
haole? How? Surely, a chute. Whoosh! Down go his clothed
plain skin and bones through a shaft to the sea.

We are all well disposed in Paradise.
Bird and flower, one. Makai or mauka,
the ocean's blue envelopes open and close
our directions. Whale bone and wisdom teeth rise
from the waves and fall, equal and queer as snow
now on the silverswords of Haleakala.

5

Crisp as coconuts and just as hairy
with the news, the operator's voice said
from the Royal Hawaiian: "Blaustein's been cancelled."
The passive voice—God, *that's* how it's done!—airs
out the room, winds up the sheets of our bare
habits, transfers the key. Maybe he never existed.
The route he's traveling into now is words.
Dead on the firmament by day, Arthur, the bear,

rises at night. And cancel is *cancelli*,
a jail or lattice, the old double-cross.
What we see through crossed fingers are the chilling
cancellations: flights, arrivals, phonings.
My hands, these rhymed lines, wave them goodbye,
linking like death and life, crossing him off.

Earth

By the time the airplane rises
I have dismantled most of Ireland,
washed the blue cemetery
smell from my heels,
folded its scrim away.

There, smaller than dung
pocked thistle, they go down
all that green rain-strung sky,
puck goat packed off, the babies
crocus white and pink as Spring.
Down Guinness, down the granite Christs
exploding from the mountainsides of accidents,
the Blessed Mother niche, down
arsenic for the fox, hawk, sheep slit still
born, all life as hard as soda bread
gnawed from a hill. Back
down the abbey-eyed wind holes where
centuries of poets pile like harps,
the dead, their lean-to
vision of the sea.

The mind is a shadowbox, a puppeteer,
and conjure as I fly the little
city hung on bridges, string
tower, bay, tunnel, seal, Presidio,
the guarding angel forward. All the props.
And further forward, Honolulu, hourly baked
sky, tin-high house,
white bikini scar that is the beach,
the yard of grave bones in the shopping mall,
mongoose shy rain and sleepy
dragon mountains all come back again.
This perfect art and mind's eye restitution
of land's end is going, going, going

underground, the rising soil
a gardener's palm is struck by,

solid loaf of roots, the stringing roads
we hold unwrapped to wild gorse
yellow fields and daffodils
that trail like plays these acts
of ours, begin and end, and every country
left behind with green.

Imagine being of the earth,
not in it.

Manoa Churchyard

Walking home from the market I can
nearly hear the crying shame of
Beloved Wife of Hung Fat Choy
at mangoes split and rotting in her soil.

My sack is filled with ginger
and kumquats, vinegar, shoyu, sugar,
Chinese five spice, and the white
plum wine she would bring to
a seasonal boil before she'd drop
the bright fruit in, but not
before taking that green thin gold
skin and meddled pink—like a trout
or a rainbow—between her teeth
to help the blade begin.

Why even now with the hot whisk of a bride
she might wind these dry fronds into a broom
and clean the whole place up!
were not her hands
swept into dust at her sides.

Elegy

We shut at night, doors latched,
world and the cat curled into corners,
dishes stacked.

The old refrigerator of the brain
shudders a moment, working,
keeping things cool,
and then the silence.

A lamp on the table in the bedroom
waits for the end of the story:

Moon hung around for a while,
a little globe,
down which the shadows moved
day after day
clearly and bound as the Sea of Cognition.

Goodnight, dear heart.

The skeleton which was a dream
wakes up and whispers.

Nothing

between us and the covers now
but morning.

For Josephine Miles

Hunger

I have opened every drawer
and cupboard I can lay my hands on
to find something of yours that is not there,
nothing but spindles of brown thread
the recluse spiders leave
behind them when they go.
No letters. No provisions.

It is always this way with want—
the palms flat as meal on the shelves
and too worn out with scarcity to make a fist.

On days when the lean malice of words
draws the rooms we walk in down
and your slow hands
fold a sheet of paper to make a window
box of blank air
I have listened—

and when an animal
rattles the dark out of its skeleton
and the wind shakes.

Love Poem

I hate to tell you, then the intern
said, *he died*. I grabbed all that I
had to wear from one hospital
to the next, my green maternity smock,
emptied the week before, a granite bucket,
a small town evacuated for the tornado,
pulled it down hard, ripcord, to take
the air I fell through, called out
anything to suck the drag of dirt
and bellyfill of gravity again.

Years and years the words come back:
when you're more calm, darling,
we'll have an autopsy, clean this mess up.
And genuflect in swathed and scrubbed
confessionals, the masks, cut skin
peeled up, pried back, strings
of intestines like blue beads to count,
to measure our Hail Marys against spleen.

You call tonight, your voice as cool
as mercury, and now the open door,
torn parachute, limelight airsuit,
the lineup buckled to the rope,
velocity, same wind, dark turbulence,
my turn to jump and

then the priest's green light is on,
and all the candles in the vestibule,
the little runway lanterns, flicker,
grow stars blown in like breath
in love, blue out, dim and more
dim the more invisible I fall.

Fool, Said My Muse

As good to write as for to lie and grone.
Astrophil and Stella

I

Said, "we're too exquisitely moral." "You, jerk, haven't
the balls to be Iseult in drag." "Never
again in marriage." Toughening with clever
lists our lips instead of longing can't
undo that later in my absent
daughter's room your mouth straightened things out. Ho, hum.
Untidy bucklings again, abdomens,
the syllables of damp predicament.

Listen, here's a list I don't need: the burn
of your internal combustion machine
at 4 a.m. Flat gin. Morality. Ice
rattling around in glasses. Listen,
the stillness in my room is clean
as water, as limes. Water and limes suffice.

William, old nut, what do you know of fret?
or convent rooms, or, for that matter, nuns?
Consider, sir, the telephone that summons
lovers to love as nuns to nones. Forget
all that claptrap about contented hermits.
Like you, he is on secular excursions,
not closeted. Were you, then, by those virgins,
waiting perhaps for hours (your head hellbent

for abbeys, theirs for prayer), glimpsed
through iron fret who, then, like startled saints
went on impossibly with their kneeling?
Dear God in heaven, I went out of this
sonnet, out of this ruled waiting for (whose name
forbidden as kiss to sisters is) his ring.

Your lady comes with flowers in my fantasy,
lavender, huddled things. I set aside
my manuscripts and offer, say, tea and bride's
cookies (an old Mexican recipe).
We settle down to Emily Dickinson
and how life's over there behind the shelf
like a slant rhyme. And the husband (the Reverend him*self*,
not that nit, Higginson) she had the crush on.

Next thing you know your wife quietly lifts the gun—
I lose my pen in the scuffle (scuffle, *hell*,
mortal, locked combat)—and fires for the throat.
Pau! All I regret as she leaves, solemn
as flowers, my desk strewn with lines I wrote
to you, is that I'm too damned dead to tell.

4

We don't speak the same language. A thing
dumb and struggled at like a gap tooth blanks
out where the dictionary was and cranks
its incommunicado tunes from gums
as flaky as erasers. My syllables—
(oh, teacher in me who says *this*, Get Down!)—
strung out on hedges of enunciation,
yours shady as an Alabama still.

Hell, that's not it, that you say baid, I bed!
If what is under us has four legs must it walk?
Language is crossing over what we said—
if *anything*—not your dark man tongue shut
of me, this white sheet lynched by sex and talk,
the Guide to Usage ripped like a pig in rut.

And you, my fair friend, sitting on the fence
of a dilapidated marriage, write
to me of the transparencies of peace. Fighting the hard lie, fighting the ten-year wrench
of word from deed, calling your wife pigwench,
mouth upside down, you say we must not bite
each time we kiss. Love is a sheer (not recondite)
vocabulary, *you* say. Priests, poets kiss peace. Hence,

Nell, this kiss of war, opaque, not see-through,
mucked, will strike the night out with its bitter wish
that rather the man would grab his sword than shoes
and fuck appearances. God, do we just *appear?*
What is apparent and transparent? This:
the guileless, flimsy, obvious, and clear.

Odi et amo . . . fieri sentio
et excrucior. Sister one minute, the next, cunt.
O drive the oxymoron to the point!
Suns splitting mountain apples on your kimono,
funky, blue soul on the radio
tell it like it is. It *is?* Please, mister, won't
you turn the up and down machine off? Why don't
you say what you mean? Earlier, an abstract ratio

laid you low on the couch. "I can't handle
the concrete," you said. Catullus—lover
of accuracy—said *nescio,* and Lesbia,
looking as lousy as I do by candle-
light probably answered: "So what else is
new with us? We contradict each other."

He at a religious dinner, saying grace
no doubt, who said he'd call. Maundy Thursday. I'm told
he's calling on God (his buddy) to behold
this burnt world with its mismatched service,
bad wine in chipped glasses through which we face
the dark not darkly now, but cracked. Were I so bold
as to imagine I were God, alone in a cold,
cracking blue, and see my lovely creature raise

his eyes, greener than psalms, than paradise,
to me, I would, after a moment's dalliance,
after the deep intake of distance
that is all life and yearning, all we praise,
grant him his every wish. Body and blood
I would break with my love to give him food.

"I dreamt he drove me back to the asylum."
The van skidded around the corner. You said,
green eyes palming again, "why are you mad?"
Beer, balked conversation, intersections,
a lost MG rankle like Thursdays on these skin-
high nerves and muscles that you've touched and startled,
felt shake, quarrel, shift, fault in this abandoned
bone house called the body. Mad, I'm not. Some-

times. Not now. The sestet is serene.
Beyond the troubling two-rhyme, the frame settles
into the composition of three plums.
Cities of refuge, possible as rain,
appear above the traffic. Language is
the House of Being, the sane say. And the poem comes.

9

Caramel as apples, her hair on your basket-
ing knees held out for windfall daughters. O and my
opposite heart, sucked like a thumb, cried
dumbly: "Me! Me! Spread, gather, tuck, comfort, catch
me to sleep!" The party circled its brass
ring around us on the floor, your fathering eyes,
as she did in your lap, resting on mine. "I've
always wanted. . . ." Did you, *I* say *that?* Some abashed

forbidden wish tree shook us down slack
that night amid the pineapples and orchids and your
daughter's tropical, flushed doze. On later ground
our laps swooned, having fallen for each other.
You now home. Still, the want stings, bites its brown,
caustic pulp on my mouth, burning like applejack.

Tree diagraming, factor trees, the tree
of life, family, language . . . I rake Sara's home
work, loose-leaf on the table, up, and we're done!
Then the forgotten outline of your body—
resolute as ironwood, limber, green
silvered needles and shivering—falls (the bone
fact of you at home) like a sudden storm
and breaks the old branch banked in history.

The trades are out of line over the entire
island tonight. Koa trunks and fallen jacaranda
uproot the volcanic earth between. An edgy
weather muddies the ground from the remembered
to the real. And the squall-lined wind of desire
blows out of its six-inch pot the Tree of Knowledge.

Heather

It is ungathered in that valley,
sprawling waves of green and lavender
like the other side of the sea
and the buds only partly broken.

In the photographs we took in the field of heather
your head keeps the direction of the shoulder,
sloped, reluctant, rather leaning toward the ground.
And my grin is stupid.

Now the cliffs are what matter and the ocean
licking around us, how it spews
fog over the road so that the minor chords
of horns rouse us from sleep. Where are we going?
The same dream of road maps hangs
its weaving in our heads.

I am going into the valley to track the white deer,
and climb down one by one my body's
rungs the lupine cliffs.
Even if my feet break, I will walk to the ocean.

Having lost love, your face, all the apparent,
necessary air, having come so far,
I will hear the rock polish of water,

draw from my flesh this bristling heather like a breath.

Gold Country

An owl, pale as down, flies out of the cedar tree,
dream from my throat, bone
nest and voice,
the red, rust center of the cedar bark howls back,
a face is ringing underwater,
and the lake where every lover stands is glass.
You say: *see what it means.*

I look for him, see how he sees
this country trail
a hand in water, leaving its touch behind
and you are when I reach
you lost in color by the river
drenched, alarmed.
In sleep and out of doors your fallen
branches fork the dry riverbed,
divine spring water.

Of course it is a dream, just as the country,
burgundy and hide, dreams mesquite,
timber, the widewale tailing wheels and shattered
brick, haze wrapped to gauze around the locust trees,
this gulch of tule fog.

Behind me the old love
draws blinds against the time of day
light smarts. Colors like old friends
are disappearing from his eyes.
He kindles envelopes. He lights a fire.

This morning we saw cypresses
yanked by their roots through iron rings
on tilted granite slabs that wrote,
their alphabet a gnarl, those buried here
are older than the hills.
Great domes of honey bloom
down at Saint Selva's Church where
Slavic patriarchs have turned to stone.

Here in Gold Country
I say *you* are my heart's breath,
the new ghost at my mouth,
this shiver steaming on the air.

My old love builds out of his hands by flame
(whose hands were
mine, whose body broke into wheat fields
the moon and *mine!*) a house of smoke.

The fires the farmers tend in the gold fields at dusk
blunder and wink like sheep.

How he stands when twilight
lowers the poppies in his garden shy as owls
I know and what it means, but not
the door he holds
or calling, *animula vagula blandula:*
come, little vagrant soul, inside.

For L. A. MacKay

Metamorphosis

The night when the silver juniper's fringe
was cover enough on the sheet,
and the long-eared owl's moon hoot
warmer than lamb's wool, and we pulled
the thermal shirts from our skins
and lay down burning for the first time
bare against the other—like a
couple of frogs, you said—
was the one night when green translations
racked my bones on the same scale,
into the same heap as yours, froglegged,
and catching your breath broke from my
blood each kelp pit, slime and lily cell,
and then a million (or a billion, is it?)
tadpoles swam in the silt once more.

Harder it is to know the women who will
wash me dead and fold these fingerwebs
of mine like wings into their pools
again than that I will not
rise from these beds.

Rite

Drawn from the *Travels of Ibn Fadlan* who visited the
encampments of the *Rus*, Swedish merchants active in the
region of the Volga, c. 922

Call me the Angel of Death (they do)
or old hag woman. My work is weaving
the doorframe the slave girl will stretch
herself over and sing. Nine days they drink
and rage, these shit-smeared warriors,
while their king turns black in the pit.
They get her ready; they pull her
by her hair and her light lips
into their tents and shove it in.
"Tell your master I did this
for love of him."

For all the dry air and the wind
hard as a hammer here in the north
a corpse won't rot but turn first
to white ash as a fire dies,
then to gray, later, darker.
Flesh is as fragile a matter as bark—
that's why we put the fruit and liquor
and the lute in with him
while he's turning in his grave.

Here are the rules: no one is chosen.
She volunteers. (Girls from good
families aren't asked.) Of course,
there is some pressure from her peers.
Even if she wanted to retract
or run away from home (some do)
we hold her to it.
A word's a word. Said's done.
This one was pretty. Not his favorite—
when the men said, "which of you will
die with him?" *she* shivered like a larch tree,
hands fallen, fallen eyes—
but younger than the others

and ready now that she had the chance
to make up for second best.

For those nine days she sang with the abandon
of a snowbird skittering on ice,
wings pucked with the glee of flight
and self-election, and the snowflakes—
such a disguise—that she would blink,
blink laughing from her eyes.
And to this day they talk of how erect
her nipples were in all the excitement.

The appointed day was clear and cold and bright.
The pine needles stood up like hairs
in a ghost story. Before sunup I
started sewing the underclothes and breeches
and caftan of silk they dressed him
in after they brushed the dirt from his skin.
Then they cut the dog in two and threw it
along with his weapons into the ship.

I've never liked this part: they take two horses
and make them gallop until they sweat,
hack them to death, fling in the pieces,
same with the two cows,
same with the cock and the hen.

We give her a drink to blur the landscape,
make a loose ladder of her bones
so that she stumbled when she
took off her ankle rings and gave them
shining in the late afternoon sun,
one to my elder daughter,
one to my younger one,
having given her arm rings to me.

We allow her one song of farewell.
Up and over the fjords she throws the light
ware of her voice. "Mother, I am coming;
Father, I am coming. Daughter I will never give,
I am coming." We allow them only one song.
The men grow restless, shift.
She is singing too long.

Inside the tent we hear the men
beating their shields with sticks
(we mustn't frighten the other girls
with her sounds) and it seems the music

calms her as I wrap the knotted cord around
her neck which is beating time
by his leathery body. She doesn't cry
when I give the ends to the men

who are standing at either side. But when
I press the knife against her heart
(O my dear, I will be quick
in finding the vital part!)

a moan uncovered by the blade's score
plucks her mouth into a flute
and she dies under my hands and in their throttle
a wild girl singing.

A wind came up after the ship
was set afire and it raged
as if the brilliant sunset weren't enough.
I heard one of our people
say to the stranger who was watching our ways.
"Your people are stupid. You take
the beloved dead and throw
them with creeping creatures into the ground.
Look at us! We burn them into paradise
in an instant!" Sure enough,

God's great breath out of the
southwest where the spring with her small,
white blossoms waits, our lady flowers,
blows the ship's timber
and my master and the slave girl into dust.

Letter

Dear God, dear mother, I am writing
from a dead room in my life, an old garage,
Manoa, falling in flats of madness
like the rain you never see,
the girls I named for horses, cows,
are husks I dropped to find some
back way back.

I open like a map your death
to get away from here.
I spread its arteries across
my lap the darkness tightens to a drum.

Something of God is here,
a piece of old male like a smell.
And sand, dust, grit: Him. Him.
What you threw out, what is a swept bouquet.

Alone it always would be this, you said,
the wind a braid the frog's voice
carries in its belly on the pond,
for hair, the plain, the needed, parting comb.

Teach me, I drum, my fingers quick, teach me
to live alone.
Teach me that rain will come
and come and that the smell, my hide,
is everywhere the stalk, the lie, the animal
that I complain.

Demeter's Lament

She lifts the pomegranate to her lips.

I gouge out pits into the sink
to build
a winter corridor of jars.

The white skulk of her teeth
lifts a strip of hide
raw as skin from the rosy bulge

and her eyes lock so hard
on blue I look over my shoulder
at the kitchen clock to find if
like the sour color of milk it tells
hazard as well as time.

Tricky as silk
her tongue stalks the yellow membrane until it
breaks like dawn or parchment
over the tight
red beads and

I shout
You know pomegranate juice stains
the counters. Take that damn thing
out of here
and eat it in the yard!

Her white shorts in the wake of my attack
sail such a sullen tilt of languor
like a vanishing ship of war

that I can rinse my anger
under the running water
and rock squat apricot
butts in the hammocks of spoons
before I think of how it
happens

cleave   and the burgeoning   the seeds

apples and onions split like thunder
in the larder and a god lays
his great darkness at her feet.

From my hands
blade, scald, preservative,
the bruised fruit

fall

sunlight over the earthquake of her
going cracks like wheat.

Martha

She is turning on the attic stairs
before me climbing Jacob's ladder out of the
white folks' anger, up to the flying squirrels
in the eaves, the downhung angel bats.
The Ouija Board has told me she is thirty-three.
I had asked for the names of my lovers,
queen to the king, who will I marry?
I asked the name of *her* lover. I AM THAT I AM
the triangled glass wrote. She is my handmaiden.
Gather the black thickets of her hair
out of her comb, build me a palace.
Make of the switch she makes you pick to strike
you with a tabernacle. That you call
her Pussy, that your mouth still smacks raise me
an altar and a sacrifice. Hers is the blood, the issue.
She is wearing starched green cotton she irons
Thursdays in the kitchen on the folding board,
cloth backed with clodbrown burns, the cloven
hoofprints of Apocalypse, my father's tread,
his shirts, his socks, ties, trousers, underwear—
lies down with such soft weight, O easy!
Jesus and the lamb a glow-worm shimmer on the wall,
stretch out our arms in starlight to the grave,
my mouth a nipple on her heart, go to my maker
when I lay this body down.

First Blood

My mother leads me to the place
exile and land the same
word that I yell three times
around her hands
as they scrape out the sand and grit
basket for my new body.

The only sound of water is my river
smell red
feather trickle dried on my ankles
a day's walk from the village
where the men close their doors
as we pass
quickly like the eyes of the dead.

Now mother says here
in the yard where the trees come to die
their old pocked tusks up
torn like the moon's dry corners
ground thin as shale
on shale of slack dust rises
where my mother beats into the hole
she makes
the thick animal
song of my entrance.

I sit down in the pool of earth
something fallen as if
my heart
to the floor of its house
she packs the dirt back
hard young solid cramped slow
tubers of blood
grow roots.

My mother braids a ring of briars
around my planted waist
ropes of smoke yank my nostrils
up as it burns

and she orders my hands
their white jutting
knuckles into mountains on the rim of the world
she creates
I am half
day night spirit half light
dark fiend matter sky ancestor half
equator grave pole.

All I
am is the other
than I am.

When the sun is swallowed and the land
lizard's tail whiffs the dark
air my mother sings
the ocean that I leave behind
me in the ground
heals the boy's humming arrow
grows our enemies
bracelets
of bright jackel teeth
is a fine net to haul rain in.

Her clean voice sweeps the door
with light I crawl
toward in my dreaming
hung through the center of the night
world to sleep
by the scorpion's thin string
the puff adder's thudding chord.

Maude's Lullaby

Your feet like startled quails at night
scatter the darkness of my room,
flourish beneath the sheet, alight,
and roost again against my womb.
Still damp with sleep your feathered hair
teases the slumber of my chin
and all the bones of my despair
are bruised beside your humid skin.
My chick, this is a barren nest,
a bed of twigs and serried leaves,
a place of dry and earnest rest.
Your hands that stir these cavities
and grope for warmth within this space
disturb the owls who will arise
to comb the shadows from your face
and rinse the dreaming from your eyes.

Sex Killer Caught in Florida

Who's this Ray guy? I yell
while she is at the mirror.
Some sweet Neopolitan treat
my daughter is: breasts
chocolate, breasts vanilla,
strawberries in the cream.
What else is news? The T.V.
tells us nine young women's
bodies have been stacking up
since May. The evidence
conflicts: stabbed here,
shot there, some strangle
held, all dead. His name
is Robert Long, not Ray.
She met him at the beach, *okay?*
She eats an apple. She has
borrowed my black shirt.
Everything I have is yours,
I sing, a song she doesn't
know. You're part of me. So
hard a part I cannot bear
to see her go. And don't forget
to write! They're only going
to the movies. Before she died
my mother lived in Florida.
I wonder if she knew this weird
guy, Long. Well, they were
prostitutes or edges of Miami's fringe. Balmy,
my daughter's seeing *Amadeus*
in Hawaii. When the twentieth concerto's
second movement starts its
fingers up the major spinal
cords, after the Requiem, before his
body piles in, is she listening
—am I—to the down here
slack, in Florida, the
minor, offbeat keys?

To My Daughter's Lover

I am a ranger at the entrance to this wilderness,
her room, these canyoned walls discolored
with the centuries of water where she sleeps,
her arm a bone, a settlement
thrown to the golden-haired stuffed animal
that caves her other pillow in.

The borderland I map, bewilderment,
is but the shadow of her bottom stones,
washed white as clouds and tender as small fish.
Her young sex tucks a paw between her legs.

If you could know her as I know her,
ranging the oakscrubbed hills where she begins,
a possum hanging from my limbs,
some light awake beyond the timberline,
if you could smell the lair we make—
leaves in their blank, damp stink,
this wind, this reeking pelt of bear—
or see the wild blue horse
flank of her hair, these campfires I call eyes,

in any dream or roundup you would know
why I drive the hard
knife of my bargain into that other
country you have come from
to notch your silver
buckled belt and drifting rawhide.

This Day in Paradise

The snake is cool and green, purled with desire
on the stalk, I tell you, inching
every which way like a woman's tongue.
I poured dirt halfway up the mountain
from my sailor hat to make the spiral stop,
clumped it flat as a carpet, when the tramp,
alert and squirrel with manners,
came out of the trees and, cap in hand,
stood for the green snake's funeral.

       In spring in West Virginia
woods fill up with laurel, dogwood, rhododendron,
sweet pinks, but he stank of gasoline, smoke, pee,
further in the twill, skunk skree. And
then the air cracks still another man,
no, let me tell you, lazy with leafsleep, said,
well sir, well sir. What we got here?
The nuns will tell you the dogwood's four-petaled
flowers are a sign of Our Savior's wounds. Ivory
curling to iron they nail His agony
upon the branch so we believe. Dumb nicotine,
dumb darkside of the moon these edges
weld to me. The trunk is shriveled, don't you see,
having been hacked up for the cross. The center
of the dogwood is the crown—tiny, punk
droppings of that one fell swoop,
passion and sacrifice.

       The tramp's nails on my shoulder
bubble the color of snot, soil in their crests
a skid of roadside snow, thief, murderer,
bedraggled spool of his mouth
all I must never speak to, speak of.
I walked down slow as smell, my shirt
blushing the flowered hills, their spewed,
demotic love, sung what I could remember,
Schlaf in himmlischer Ruh. The road snaked.
Home is there, after dark, after the punishment.

Seized, Jesus-rattled—what do I know?—
Luther cried: "The world is a turd
hanging from the asshole of God!"
And Saint Anne, her lips turned into parable,
teaches the Virgin to read
as I would spell you loving out of my arms
mornings like this, your eyes, their blue and sleeping
grass, these snowdrops, dirt high,
just beginning, skittish at daybreak,
cold as a witch's tit, wear for an amulet:
the devil's prick is an icicle.

    O holy and minute particulars,
this opening, wet earth, lochia, located,
placenta, placed, I say, our world, not *shat,*
its blue, uncut umbilical of stars!—
twisting and twisting out of the northeasterly
air over the deltas, over the lowered savannas,
over the slow, sidewinding slough of the surf
at Mokole'ia where his young and white and strapping
fingers bind her throat, filled with his semen,
filling with seafoam, her mouth salt and
yelling for her father, yelling for her father,
seeing in the southern sky, child-wide and
yelling for her father, that half-cocked crux,
one star yanked up and sucking blackness as far away
as the hand of salvation from her forehead.

For Maile Gilbert (1980–1985)

Haworth Parsonage, 31 March 1855*

Literature cannot be the business of a woman's life, and it ought
not to be. The more she is engaged in her proper duties, the less
leisure will she have for it, even as an accomplishment and a
recreation. To those duties you have not yet been called, and when
you are, you will be less eager for celebrity. You will not seek in
imagination for excitement, of which the vicissitudes of this life,
and the anxieties from which you must not hope to be exempted,
be your state what it may, will bring with them but too much."

Letter from Robert Southey to Charlotte Brontë, March 1832

I

At Bridlington when I saw it for the first time
the slam of that adamant,
unbridled hand at my feet pounding No!
threw pieces of white water over my hem
like torn paper,
but my shoes held fast under the sinking
heave of the shingle that soaked clear
to the shores of my heels. Oh, wild
and dear
God! The sea!

      In Haworth the winds
shock burls of leaves abruptly into the winter
light like scrolls of birds
and we all waver a little under our skins;
and then back from a walk on the moors,
an odd, vagrant squall, queer as a gypsy, might knock
us into one another, ripping the sheer lace
of the waterfall
to shreds against the rock.

      But this slate-blue, complete, hurled
water's refusal. No blind rider is so hard in falling.

I never mended well
or governed the children's minds and bones smartly;

*The day Charlotte Brontë, eighteen-months married, two-months
pregnant, died.

their call from the banister
fell always on the other side of that estate
where I lived what I dreamed of
and not the position I held,
and my vision so impaired that in my employment
at Stonegappe I had
to bend for the needle's squint against the candle flame,
and listen to the diastolic clench
of Mrs. Sidgwick's breath in the room's small air
beat its shallow envy against whichever
neighbor's wall was higher.

Oh God, you send the sea to tell us: No
Trespassing. There are billows of gray and thick
weather in this atmosphere where we are told
not to go. Restrain, these furious breakers claim,
your trying, protestant
heart. This is the order of things.

My eyes like old women
who cannot leave their neighborhoods
saw the rain-silk layers of water
under my skirt
vanish like shot silver into the edge of the land,
saw the Yorkshire coast sail from the straw
harbor of my bonnet over the rim of the fallow world
toward Brussels and London, and then my name—
or was it his?—balance like a single
buoy in the channel.

Later I would learn from Mr. Thackeray that the sublime
means only until the limits: a boundary held
between water and settlement, hearth and the moderate air
that the rampage cannot cross.
Order thrust to its very limits and no
farther is sublime. A woman writing, a woman living
two persons at once, female and male, the bondage
broken, the water's fist grinding aside the sea wall,
banked coals ruptured by a spinster's throat into flares
is the verge of a terrible
creation that annihilates its frame.

The second time I saw it on our wedding trip
to County Clare when Arthur let me,
wrapped in his husbanding rug,
not look so far over the cliff to be chilled by the spray,
nor close enough at the rocks
to engage as I had at Bridlington
my skirts in that clash of sea water with the land and its
inhabitants—hung
cormorant over the coast,
I felt the solution of blood and the bitter sea
liquid within me
begin.

      Launched with no warning
out of my cells, the small craft
was a secret in January as I walked with Arthur
on the moor to the falls and saw
like a bride's veil worn to threads,
its intricate fret unwoven on the wind's loom,
the snow melted as if by furnaces to a clear, stinging vapor
white as the fibers of wedding cloth
Glauce tried to strip from her poisoned skin
or, under the rain that followed us home,
so it appeared,
and I caught cold.

For ten days the winds of the equinox
have surged and crashed like bores against the uncompliant
stones of this parsonage. The shelves in the churchyard
crack in vernal heaving every year, break half and half,
splitting the dead world open.
This is the uproar nature orders in seasons
of revolution when day and night
are briefly equal, as if parity
were a sphere to be thrashed out of the universe.
And I am bound in that direction.

Over the surface of things—
the quilt stitch, the benefice
of vellum lamplight, the Book of Common Prayer—
Arthur kneels and casts his imprecations
into the flood of my refusal
like a net,

> *We beseech thee to loose*
> *the spirit of this thy*
> *servant from every bond*

and hears
hurled from a woman's precipice
over the birth caul,
over the skull cap knitting its hard
adhesion to the brain,
my No! that will take the water
of the shale-gray tides in my voice down with me—
the sea, its passengers and creatures,
poured back like a libation on the land:
feather, scale, cartilage, fontanel,
the fountain flowing over
underground.

Not to see the sea again, not to bear the sea rain
down but the branches of sea trees,
to grow its deep and savage
weeds below the roots of civil grain—
The tremors under your walk will be my words,
the fissure in the soil
cracking your summer garden like a snake,
my son or daughter. On the horizon rockets
of virulent, scalding minerals will break
the ultramarine lintel of the sky,
the surface of the earth's threshold burst
with the eruption of sea
water
finding its level.

Letter to Karma

This page sunlit and blinding, I look down at the mall,
the hotels, the beach long as an airstrip where you sprawl,

the following sea your skin can cut a fast
lane through as if water were only the grass

we have remembered barefoot, green: you the
melodic stride of women in my dreams.

The piano quartet in C minor Beethoven
composed when he was fifteen (youth proven

not all bad) is stringing beads of amber on the air.
What divides us like continents is your slant that fear

to love is warning, not blandishment. You, my slow,
silly dear, wet from the roughwater swim of love, should know

better, though your heart is still that side of the reef
where we there see nothing is other than death.

Impatient with Kate Chopin's surfaces, at the beach
Thursday you bucked your hair and said: "I want to teach

lines told by the dying and the very old."
And your voice leaned for a moment over the narrow

balcony of its bones as if in the salt light
of afternoon you had no fear of heights

or of my fathoming glance: a woman
on the brink of what has happened and what might. Then

read Mona Van Duyn's poems if you dare
on sex after sixty, parents in their last years.

Look the square mother of me in the eye,
and teach me like a sophomore how to die.

Fear is the reason to love, its path. When
twice I stood, hating to venture in,

hating the way each man turned toward a lost wall,
on the doorsill of dying, fear was the hall

way behind me, the alarmed corridor, not where,
in love, I had to go, only what got me there.

On Saturdays like this while planes fly
darts of silver hope into the journey's bullseye,

and Brahms in old age tracks the cello down,
and even Scotch is harmless; while, long and brown,

you lie matted with sunlight on the sand,
I know that what you said was right. On the other hand,

like glinting shoals, or a gold pool, your breast
bone, or the searching sweatband of your eyes, honest

but not true. Under the blue school of meaning slips
the electric eel, glare, sharp, an arrow, toughlipped,

edgewise and ancient, always there, the singing
leer of terror I could hide, knowing

that I might keep your cruel innocence alive
and win your love, Karma, if I would lie

to you. But I don't. Fear tries the strong heart,
hardens it, slaps it around like a glove, is martial art:

the first heat, the last handicap of love.

Vision

Husband, you come still against the window,
your bookpack like the old days filled with Descartes
and Hobbes, that rakish cap, moth-shadowed, slung
along the left side of the blood
bruised eye we wandered over all Manhattan
for a doctor to set right, then

took the Circle-the-Island Cruise. I kissed that far sight's
gray and leveled edges. How the city must
have looked to you! Splattered, spread
out in filigrees of red, the slow East River's
damaged artery pumping us
down, bright scarlet prints held up, their fingers
frisked and wild, on every tenement
a sunset struggled. The doctor said

"you'll live," putting the drops in. Just what happened
puzzled us. Sometimes, he mused, a speck
comes out of nowhere, bang, a vessel breaks,
the damaged bird of eye
sinks into other colors, dragonflied, beats
magnified, stained wings into a screen someone has closed,
is gone. But not the bloodshot drumming.

THE
JUNIPER
PRIZE

This volume is the fourteenth recipient
of the Juniper Prize
presented annually by the
University of Massachusetts Press
for a volume of original poetry.
The prize is named in honor of
Robert Francis (1901–87),
who lived for many years at
Fort Juniper, Amherst, Massachusetts.